J
FIC
ROSS   Ross, Sylvia

Lion Singer

DUE DATE

LION SINGER

WRITTEN AND ILLUSTRATED BY
SYLVIA ROSS

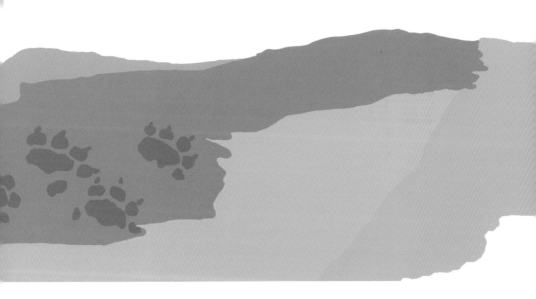

HEYDAY BOOKS
BERKELEY, CALIFORNIA
GREAT VALLEY BOOKS

Heyday Books, founded in 1974, works to deepen people's understanding and
appreciation of the cultural, artistic, historic, and natural resources of California
and the American West. It operates under a 501(c)(3) nonprofit educational organi-
zation (Heyday Institute) and, in addition to publishing books, sponsors a wide
range of programs, outreach, and events.

To help support Heyday or to learn more about us, visit our website at
www.heydaybooks.com, or write to us at P.O. Box 9145, Berkeley, CA 94709.

Library of Congress Cataloging in Publication Data:
Ross, Sylvia.
  Lion Singer / Sylvia Ross.
      p. cm.
  Summary: In long-ago California in the area populated by the various tribes of
the Yokuts group, Dog Cry, a young Chukchansi Indian boy, saves his little sister
from a mountain lion and gains a new name.
  ISBN 1-59714-009-0 (hardcover : alk. paper)
  1. Yokuts Indians--Juvenile fiction. [1. Yokuts Indians--Fiction. 2. Indians of
North America--California--Fiction. 3. Brothers and sisters
--Fiction. 4. California--History--To 1846--Fiction.] I. Title.
  PZ7.R7199125Lio 2005
  [Fic]--dc22

                                                    2004029314

Book design by Rebecca LeGates

Orders, inquiries, and correspondence should be addressed to:
  Heyday Books
  P.O. Box 9145
  Berkeley, CA 94709
  (510) 549-3564; Fax (510) 549-1889
  heyday@heydaybooks.com

Printed in Thailand by Imago

10 9 8 7 6 5 4 3 2 1

This book is dedicated to all the children of
Chukchansi descent in Madera County, to the children
of the Tule River Indian Reservation in Tulare County,
and to our grandchildren who carry a little bit of Native
California into the future with them—Stephanie, Ryan,
Sarah, Sydney, and Drew Ross.

PRONUNCIATION GUIDE

Tsuloniu (Tsu-lo-nee-oo)
Suksanau (Suk-sa-na-oo)
Apasau or Hapasau (Ah-pah-sah-oo)
Kataniu (Ka-ta-nee-oo)

There was once a time when there was no metal in the Chukchansi people's world. There was no metal, so there were no clocks or frying pans. There were no barbecue grills. There were no cars. There were no wristwatches or television sets. There was not one single nail in the land of the Chukchansis. Even if there had been metal to make soda cans, no one had invented soda. The Chukchansis drank cool water from rivers and streams when they were thirsty.

Of course, back then there were no white people on this side of the mountains. There were no black people either. The mountains to the east were so high that buffalo and horses had never crossed them to come to the hill country of the Chukchansi. Far to the west, across California's great valley, stories were told of strange pale people who came and brought odd animals to the Ohlone people of the coastal lands. But swamps covered the valley between the Chukchansi people and the

Ohlone people, so those strange people with their strange animals had never come to the Chukchansi villages of Tsuloniu, Kataniu, Apasau, and Chikchanan.

In the land of the Chukchansi there were no cows, but there were deer, antelope, and mountain sheep. There were no chickens, but there were quail, blue jays, hawks, and eagles.

While there were no horses or buffalo, there were great herds of elk grazing in the valleys. Two kinds of bears lived in the hills and hollows. The rivers that flowed down to the valley were home to silvery fish, clams, and crawdads.

The Chukchansi shared all these good things of the earth with their neighbors to the north, the Miwok, and their cousins, the other Yokuts to the south.

It was a good place to live.

The Chukchansi people had four big villages: Tsuloniu, Kataniu, Apasau, and Chikchanan. Three or four times a year, the members of the tribe got together and had a campout. Sometimes the campout would be in one village, and sometimes it would be in another.

When the villages got together, the children could run free because their families were busy planning songs and dances and making food. Sometimes when the adults were busy the children got into trouble. But usually they were good.

Chukchansi teenagers were supposed to watch the medium-sized children. Medium-sized children were supposed to watch the little children. No one had to watch the Chukchansi babies, because they were in cradleboards and their mothers took care of them.

One summer there was a big campout in the village of Apasau. Dog Cry was a medium-sized boy. He came from the village of Kataniu, where his mother's clan lived. He

was happy to be at the summer campout because he could run and play with his cousins, who lived in the other villages. The cousins who lived in Apasau knew all the secret places around the village. They knew places where children could go and no one would bother them.

Dog Cry was supposed to watch his little sister while all the grownups were busy setting up camp. But his cousins called to him, and he decided to play with them in the oak woods beyond the camp. His little sister, who was called Breaks Shells, began to follow him. Dog Cry wanted to be with his cousins, so he took her hand and led her back to the camp to the place where the elders sat in the shade. He thought that the elders would take care of her so he would be free to play with his cousins.

When Breaks Shells saw her great-grandmother, she ran on her fat little legs and jumped into the old woman's lap. Dog Cry was free! He quickly ran away before Great-grandmother could call him back.

Dog Cry's cousins were waiting for him on the path in the meadow. They were acting rowdy and silly and told him about a special place at the top of a hill. The hill rose at the far end of the campground and was taller than the other hills around the meadow. The boys followed the meadow path. It led past some big berry bushes. Behind the berries there was a gully where winter rains sometimes made a creek. In the summer it was wide and dry, and the boys tried to jump across. On the other side, the cousins began to climb the hill that rose just beyond the gully's edge.

They climbed until they came to a place where rocks had long ago come down and made a big sloping pile on the steep hillside. Cousin Flea broke a short branch from a small oak tree and the other boys did the same. The boys knew to scrape the branches on the rocks in front of them as they climbed across the rock fall.

Nassis, the rattlesnake, lived in the rocks and the cousins wanted to warn him that they were climbing through his land. Even though Nassis was a creature of great power, he was very shy. When he heard the branches scraping, he would slip away.

The boys' mothers had taught them this when they were very small. No Chukchansi woman would cross through rocks or go off a path without a branch in her hand to warn Nassis. It was polite to warn Nassis if you were coming to a place where he lived.

Cousins were the best thing in Dog Cry's life, because he had no brothers. His father's older wife had three girls, and his mother, the younger wife, had only Dog Cry and his little sister. In his home village of Kataniu, Dog Cry had many friends, but they were not the same as cousins.

The boys scrambled up and over the rock pile and found themselves high on a ledge overlooking the whole campground. Far down below them, Dog Cry and his cousins could see their fathers with the men from all the Chukchansi villages. The men were building shelters, fishing, and clearing a place for the singing and dancing later that evening. The boys could see the women building a long cooking fire and they could hear the laughing of the women in the camp. Dog Cry looked down to the long shelter where the elders sat in the shade. He saw Great-grandmother, but he didn't see his sister.

He called to him. They were laughing again as they raced each other, climbing further up the hill. The oldest cousin was called Always Angry, though his full name was The Boy Who Is Always Angry. He seldom spoke and almost never smiled. Always Angry grabbed a knotty little tree and pulled himself up a cliff until he was two man-lengths above the other boys. Dog Cry wanted to climb with them, but he was worried. He didn't know where his sister was.

He looked carefully at the elders as they sat talking. He still could not see his sister. He could see where the women of four villages were preparing food. He could see his mother lift her cooking basket and go toward the fire. Breaks Shells was not with her. He saw his older sisters giggling and talking together. Breaks Shells was not with them.

Looking down at the camp, he could see the narrow path where he had run to meet his cousins. It ran from the campground across the meadow to the bottom of the hill. He saw the dry meadow grass all yellow in the sun.

Far from the elders, far from the campground and deep in the meadow, he saw his sister. The little girl was trudging along, moving farther and farther away from the safety of camp. She was following him. Her black hair shined against the dry yellow grasses as she came closer to the berry bushes at the bottom of the hill.

Dog Cry was annoyed. Why did she always want to follow him? He didn't want to have to go down and take her back to camp. He wanted to climb higher with his cousins. Cousin Flea was already high above him. They would climb to the top without him. He began to climb again.

Dog Cry was thinking about what he should do. He thought about how small Breaks Shells was. She was too big for a cradleboard, but too small to have any sense. Maybe she would turn back. He knew he should wait and watch to make sure she turned back. He went back and sat on the ledge, watching her, letting his legs dangle over the edge.

The air up on the hill smelled good, of sun and dust. There was a clean mineral smell coming from the granite

rock pile he had crossed. The oak leaves around him had their own tree-in-summer smell.

His cousins were far above him now. Flea was jumping around and knocked some pebbles down on him. "Come on," the boys called. Always Angry waved down to him and pointed up even higher, showing him where the cousins were going to climb next.

Dog Cry looked down and saw Breaks Shells coming closer to the berry bushes. She was not turning back. Her tiny feet moved her closer to the bottom of the hill. Her hair swung as she moved along.

As he watched her, he saw a long, strange shadow in the gully at the bottom of the hill. The shadow wasn't the color of berry-bush shadows. Instead, it was a dull tan color. Then the strange shadow moved. But there was no wind.

Dog Cry couldn't believe what he saw. Crouched in the cover of the berry bushes at the edge of the gully was a great, tawny mountain lion, bigger than a man. Breaks Shells was moving in her steady way closer and closer to it.

Dog Cry didn't know what to do. Worried thoughts came swirling through his mind and filled it up.

Lions had more power than Nasis. The spirit of a lion was cunning and bold. His grandfather had told him that only a grizzly bear had a strong enough spirit to challenge a lion. Dog Cry just stared down at his sister and the great cat waiting for her. On the other side of the berry bushes, Breaks Shells took two more steps along

the path. She was moving toward the lion. Dog Cry's mind settled and he knew what he had to do.

The boy jumped up screaming out his loudest and shrillest cry. He screamed out so loudly that Breaks Shells could hear him. The whole camp could hear him. His cousins heard him. Even the great crouched lion heard him and looked up toward the hillside and snarled. The lion's big teeth shone white in the shadows of the gully. But then he moved his great shoulders, and his paws inched closer to the place where the path went around the berries, the place where Dog Cry's sister was walking.

Dog Cry couldn't wait for his cousins or for the people of the villages. He began to run down the hill as fast as he could run. He was running to his sister. Going faster and faster, he thought he might trip when he came to the rock fall. But he could not stop. If he could make himself a target, the lion might ignore Breaks Shells.

He ran down so fast it felt like he was flying. His feet barely touched the hard surface of the steep, sloping rock pile. He didn't worry about Nassis. He didn't even worry about the claws or teeth of the lion. He worried about nothing but running down the hill as fast as he could.

Dog Cry's toes skidded in the dirt beyond the rocks. He started to slide in the soft dust and leaves, but caught himself and continued racing downhill. He was swift and fleet. His own spirit wanted to call to the spirits of elk and deer to help him, but he knew that elk and deer never run toward danger. He did not think they would help him run toward the lion.

But his spirit called to them anyway.

He prayed that although elk and deer did not have courage, they would give him their speed. Elk and deer did help him, for suddenly he found himself at the bottom of the hill and on the edge of the gully. He came to a stop just across from the great tan beast and he saw its yellow eyes and long white fangs. He saw its sharp claws.

Breaks Shells came around the berry bushes and saw her brother and the lion. The mountain lion shook his smooth head, and his ears grew flatter. His eyes narrowed and he snarled at the little girl. He snarled at Dog Cry for interfering. He looked from Breaks Shells to her brother, then back at her. The lion began to inch toward the little girl.

Dog Cry screamed again and again. He put both his arms up in the air as high as he could reach. He shook his snake stick at the lion. The lion turned his head toward him.

Dog Cry didn't have time to be afraid. A feeling came into his throat and he began to make up a song. Instead of screaming he sang, "Ta ne, ta ne we he sit." He sang as loudly as he could. "Ta ne, ta ne we he sit." As he jumped into the gully, the boy grabbed at a broken berry vine. He didn't even notice that its stickers punctured his hand. He waved the vine at the lion with one hand and his snake stick with the other. He moved toward the lion, singing.

More song words came to him and he sang, "Hi ama wok ye. Hi ama wok ye la pa he. Ta ne, ta ne we he sit."

He knew that the lion was bigger than his father and his claws were sharper than spears. He knew the lion could kill him as easily as it killed a deer or coyote. He danced in front of the lion, waving the vine. He sang his best song, as loud as he could.

The cousins on the hillside behind him came sliding and tumbling down. Cousin Flea was yelling, and the cousins were all shouting so loudly that the birds had left the oak trees and flown to the meadow. All the people from the camp began to run across the meadow to see what the commotion by the berry bushes was all about.

The big lion watched the boy switching the air and moving toward him. The lion heard the Chukchansi song coming from the boy's mouth. Dog Cry's cousins heard his song too, and they joined in his singing. "Hi ama wok ye la pa he. Ta ne, ta ne we he sit," the cousins sang.

The cousins began to grow bolder. They jumped across the gully and clustered behind Dog Cry. They waved their sticks and broken branches. They threw small rocks and chunks of dirt at the lion. The boys jumped up and down and made fierce faces. They shrieked and yelled and sang, "Ta ne, ta ne we he sit."

Lion did not like Dog Cry's singing. He did not like the cousins' singing either. His powerful claws and sharp fangs could rip into all the children, but the singing hurt his ears. Lion flattened his ears back on his head so he wouldn't hear Dog Cry's song. Slowly, the great cat began to retreat from the noise. With his shoulders still crouched and his tail twitching, the lion moved backward, away from Dog Cry and the boys. Suddenly he turned and ran. He disappeared into the shrubbery by the river.

Breaks Shells was safe. The boys were safe. Dog Cry thanked the spirits of elk and deer that had helped him run down the hillside. He thanked the spirits of the ancestors of the Chukchansi who had given him courage and his song. He thanked the spirit of the lion for going away.

Breaks Shells had tears on her face as she looked across the gully to the boys. Cousin Flea began to laugh. "You are a hero, Dog Cry," he said. All the boys began to laugh. They didn't know why they were laughing.

Breaks Shells didn't know why her brother and her cousins were laughing either, but the laughing made her tears come faster. Her face was dusty and her fat cheeks had wet tracks down them. Dog Cry picked her up and held her. She was alive. She was safe.

The people of the four villages had all come running down the path. They reached the berry bushes and saw the children. Men and women came. Teenagers came. Even the elders came down to the berry bushes to see what was going on, but of course the elders came more slowly.

When she had pushed through the crowd, Dog Cry's mother took Breaks Shells into her arms, and she asked Dog Cry what had happened. But everyone was talking at once. The air around the berry bushes had never been so full of questions. Dog Cry had no voice left. He couldn't answer his mother.

But all the cousins began to answer and to tell the story. Of course Cousin Flea's voice was the loudest. Flea told how his cousin from the village of Kataniu, his cousin who was named Dog Cry, had saved little Breaks Shells by chasing a huge mountain lion away. But no one believed Cousin Flea. The other cousins tried to tell the story but the people from the four villages all shook their heads in doubt. The cousins knew no one believed them. "There was no lion," someone said.

Flea's father said that a lion would never come so close to camp. The most elder of the elders of Tsuloniu, the largest village of the Chukchansi, frowned. He wanted to know why a little girl had wandered so far from camp. "Who was watching this little granddaughter?" he asked, scowling at the boys.

One bad-tempered man Dog Cry knew from the village of Kataniu said, "You scared a bobcat, not a lion. You boys disturbed camp for nothing." He spit on the ground. The faces of many people relaxed. They were relieved. No one wanted to believe a lion had come so close to camp.

Always Angry, the oldest of the cousins, stepped forward. In a big voice, he spoke loudly to the crowd. "My cousin from the village of Kataniu fought a lion, not a bobcat. We know what bobcats look like and we know what lions look like."

He looked straight at the men and the elders. "This was a lion," he said slowly and clearly. "A great tan lion. It was fierce. It was as big as a man and it had fangs as long as a man's hand. It was lying in the gully here behind the berries. It was waiting for Breaks Shells. It would have killed her. Maybe it would have killed all of us. Dog Cry fought it with only a berry vine and a stick in his hands."

The headman of Apasau, host of the summer camp, frowned and stepped down into the shallow gully. The people of the four villages of the Chukchansi watched as he carefully examined the ground in the shade of the berry bushes. Then he turned to the people. He held his hand up so everyone would be quiet.

"People," he said, "The Boy Who Is Always Angry is my son. He does not speak unless he has something to say. He told us that Dog Cry frightened a lion. We don't want to believe that a lion came so close to camp. But this was not a bobcat. This was a lion, a very large lion." He pointed to the soft dirt at the edge of the gully closest to the berry bushes. "Look," he said, "Its tracks are here in the dust."

The headman of Apasau smiled at the boys. "A bobcat does not have feet bigger than a man's hand," he said. The headman held up his left hand and spread the fingers wide apart. "A bobcat's body is not longer than a man's body." He looked at the people with a serious face.

"What these boys say is the truth. This boy from the village of Kataniu is a boy not yet big enough to go on a hunt or even into a sweat lodge with men. But he drove away a lion with a berry vine."

Flea couldn't be completely still while the headman of Apasau, the host of the whole summer camp, was speaking. Cousin Flea interrupted to say, "Dog Cry didn't scare away the lion with a berry vine. He scared the lion away with his singing." This, of course, made all the people laugh. The headman and the most elder of all the elders laughed too.

Dog Cry's mother held Breaks Shells up for everyone to see. She looked at her daughter and her son and smiled. Dog Cry looked at her and he knew she was happy with him. His father stood in the crowd and he too looked at his son. Dog Cry knew his father was proud of him on this day.

The headman of Apasau, host of the summer campout for four villages, held up both hands and the crowd quieted down. He straightened up and waited until even the babies and little children became quiet, and the elders had stopped grumbling.

Then the headman of Apasau looked over at the old man who was the most elder of the elders of Tsuloniu, the largest village of the Chukchansi, and they solemnly nodded to each other.

The most elder of the elders of Tsuloniu, the largest village of the Chukchansi, spoke to Dog Cry. "From this day," he said, "You are no longer the boy called Dog Cry. You will be known by a new name. From this day, you are to be called Lion Singer. The old man turned to the people and added, "A boy by the name of Lion Singer has brought honor to all the villages of the Chukchansi tribe on this day."

The Chukchansi people all smiled as they turned and walked back to camp. Many people reached out to softly touch Lion Singer's back or arm as they passed him. None of the tribe's people ever scolded Lion Singer for having left his sister. The people saw Lion Singer with his mother and his sister and they knew he had already learned enough. The Chukchansi people were very, very wise. They did not say what did not need to be said.

As they walked back, Lion Singer began having proud thoughts. He even had the proud thought that one of the

tribe's storytellers might make a story-song about him in camp that night.

While the boy called Lion Singer was having proud thoughts, the boy who was once called Dog Cry was thinking serious thoughts. He was very glad he had cousins. They had bravely helped him fight a lion. He knew he had needed their help and they had come to help him. He thought that cousins were nearly the best thing in his life.

He knew a little sister was the very best thing in his life.

THINGS CHUKCHANSI CHILDREN SHOULD
KNOW AND REMEMBER

The Chukchansi tribe had many villages and were a peaceful people who spoke a language related to the languages of the other Yokuts people of California and of the Nez Perce tribe of Idaho. The four main Chukchansi villages were on the south side of what is now called the Fresno River. Highest up in the hills were Tsuloniu (Tsu-lo-nee-oo), near the headwaters of Picayune Creek, and Chikchanan, also called Suksanau (Suk-sa-na-oo), on the Fresno River. Further downstream and closer to the valley were Apasau, also called Hapasau (Ah-pah-sah-oo), situated in Fresno Flats, now Oakhurst, and Kataniu (Ka-ta-nee-oo), in the region of the present-day Picayune Rancheria.

Nassis is the Chukchansi word for rattlesnake.

We he sit means "mountain lion."

Ta ne (or *ha ne*) means "Go away."

Hi ama wok ye la pa he means "This one gives the whip."

TRIBAL HISTORY

The Chukchansi were the most northern tribe of the large Yokuts group of Native Californians. The Yokuts were not a tribe themselves, but were an assembly of tribes who spoke related languages and shared many customs.

The Chukchansi settled the hill country in what is today eastern Madera County thousands of years ago. They traded with the Miwok and Maidu, with the eastern Shoshone-Paiutes, called the Monache, and sometimes with other Yokuts tribes to the west and south.

These tribes were rich in the things people needed to have good lives. With plentiful game, hunting was easy. Squirrel, rabbit, possum, porcupine, deer, elk, and both brown and grizzly bears provided ample meat, and also the leather and furs needed to make comfortable clothing and other household items. The large stands of many varieties of oak trees provided acorns that were harvested in the fall and made into meal.

Nature also provided edible insects, birds, and fish. Many kinds of native berries, nuts, and fruits were used to flavor and preserve food.

The climate was very mild. The winters were short and rainstorms seldom lasted more than two or three days at a time. Spring came early and the weather was warm most of the year. The Chukchansi and their Yokuts neighbors were among the most peaceful people of North America. Hostility among the Yokuts tribes was virtually unknown.

Change came in the mid 1700s, when Spanish soldiers and missionaries began to recruit and sometimes enslave the Indians of the southern California coast. Traders carried knowledge of these foreign people, but for about a hundred years, very few white people came into central California.

Then gold was discovered at a small white settlement in Nisenan territory in 1848. It is estimated that by 1850 one hundred thousand white gold seekers filled every creek and stream throughout the lands of the foothill tribes. The gold miners invaded the territories of the Maidu, Konkow, Nisenan, Miwok, and Chukchansi. Greed for gold prompted the Mariposa Indian Wars in 1851. This open annihilation of the Native hill people of California was preceded by a court ruling that no Indian could testify in court against a white person—a ruling that in effect made it legal to murder Indians.

The death rate was so great that historians estimate the tribal population of California dropped more than 85 percent during the decades between 1850 and 1880.

Adult Chukchansi were shot on sight. Chukchansi children were bought and sold to work for miners and settlers. Homes were burned and even foundation stones were broken apart. The few people who escaped slaughter scattered throughout the hill country and tried to survive however they could, wherever they could find refuge.

The nineteenth century brought devastation to the Chukchansi. The twentieth century brought little better. Most Chukchansi, resisting the government's attempt to move them to distant reservations, were plagued by the diseases brought by contact with the white man: tuberculosis, alcoholism, and diabetes caused by the white culture's refined sugar and flour.

But by 1900, a few families had reestablished their residences by land grant in the area of Coarsegold. In the late 1920s, a number of Chukchansi were bold enough to register as Indians and proclaim their tribal lineage. Finally, in 1994—more than sixty years later—the government officially recognized the Picayune Rancheria of Chukchansi Indians in Coarsegold, which made them eligible to receive health care, grants, and other benefits. Chukchansi people, long scattered, were at last able to gather together and become a viable tribe. Now, in the twenty-first century, the Chukchansi have a hopeful future: while the tribe cannot regain the lifestyle of long ago, its members are at last empowered to step beyond the horrors of the past two hundred years.

AUTHOR'S NOTE

Kathleen Simpson, the former administrator of the Picayune Rancheria of Chukchansi Indians, had been encouraging me for a while to combine my experience with children and my interest in writing. She wanted me to write something that would incorporate the history of the tribe into stories for the contemporary tribe's children.

This book is the result of that encouragement. It is set in an earlier time and in the landscape of our tribal area, where my grandmother and great-grandmother were born. This is the foothill country of eastern Madera County.

But the essence of the story comes from years of watching California Indian children in the classroom and at play on the Vandalia schoolyard near the Tule River Indian Reservation. The children I taught were strongly bonded with their siblings and cousins. They looked out for each other. The responsibility shown by older children for younger ones crossed the boundaries of age and gender and was touching to witness. These experiences inspired this book.

Great Valley Books is an imprint of Heyday Books, a nonprofit publishing company based in Berkeley, California. Created in 2002 with a grant from the James Irvine Foundation and with the support of the Great Valley Center (Modesto, California), the Great Valley series strives to publish, promote, and develop a deep appreciation of various aspects of the region's unique history and culture. We are grateful to James McClatchy for his support of this volume.

GREAT
VALLEY